Rush

Of

Many

Waters

Also by Pauly Hart

Rush of Many Waters:

Volume Ten

By Pauly Hart

ISBN: 978-1-955399-14-2
Library of Congress Catalog Data is available at: Loc.gov
This book is available at cost on Amazon.com and wherever
fine books are sold.
Any references to historical events, real people, or real
places are used fictitiously. Names, characters, and
places are products of the author's imagination.
Front Cover Art by Franz Marc:
Front cover design by Pauly Hart
Paperback version printed in Savannah, Georgia, USA,
where available.
First Edition, 2021
Author Contact: EmpiresAndGenerals@gmail.com
Author Website: PaulyHart.com

Contents

Alabaster Coin

J'ka fumbled the alabaster coin in his fingers, not knowing what it was. Kir, the elder-tech, had given it to him earlier that day in the long hallway that lead to Kir's office. Kir and J'ka both worked at Frabow Tech. Lately they had been working on some strange new developments on the Magnetic Flux Generator.

"Take it J'ka! And shut up about it! I don't care where you hide it! I don't want to know. Just do not let Litmat know that you have it." Then he looked around, cursed and walked down the hallway in the other direction.

J'ka had spent the rest of the day working quietly in his terminal reviewing the gene specs for the endocrine drive of a Magflux stimulator. The stimulator had promised an 80% increase in productivity among the android operators of Magflux portals. This had been a big thing. Androids of the thinkbot level were mainly used in Portal control, and that was where Frabow made all of its Tix. According to the company, the love of Tix was the root of all kinds of evil. Coincidently, the employees of Frabpow never saw of the wonderful profits that the company made.

J'ka was actually done with his project. He had been done for two DIVs, but the company had an allotment for four on this project, and since it had only taken him one DIV to complete it, he had three to burn. So many allotments for so many hours, and he was required to be there for all of his. The day had come to an end, and he had headed home.

Putting the coin back into his pocket, he got off the tram. This was his stop, and though he hadn't punched the button, the driver knew enough to let him off there.

"Smart aleck computer." J'ka muttered, and watched it pull away.

J'ka was a mellow sort. Nothing much fazed him. Even earlier that year, when his partner had left him for a different city, he had responded with: "Have fun".

He walked the small walk home to his scraper. It wasn't much. Only seventy stories... One of the small ones on the superblock, but still it was home. He lived on floor fifty nine, unit fifteen west.

Up the lift. Taggers with decks had sprayed the whole inside with a mod for a First Person Shooter Game. Whoever got into the lift had a reading taken of them, and their image was imported into the FPS. Not realizing that they were part of the game, it was hilarious to the players to have random people popping in for them to blast. *Zam! Zam! Zam!* The lase-tags blasted into J'ka's image. *Blam!* His screen lit up with "Level Over! Zero Kills! You Suck!" and went black. When the lift came to a stop at 23 for another passenger, both of them were now thrust into the game with the same result. The other passenger stood there and sighed.

"When did they do this?" J'ka asked the man.

"Must have been last night. They've been playing all day. The techboys on floor three did it up. Been having a LAN party all day with it. You would think it gets boring after a while, but the super picked it up, and is now broadcasting scores on the interwebs... Sorry." He managed a smile as the lift stopped at J'ka's floor.

Floor three was where the techboys lived. Mostly neophytes who holed up into microunits and lived out of their boxes thru their decks. A standard apartment, the size of J'ka's would be able to support two or three, if it was a small child, but their microunits were 1/12th the size... Just big enough to install a reclino and a good deck, but not a toilet. Most of the dedicated techboys had catheters anyway and a steady stream of nurses who checked on them. J'ka had thought about it before... Living like they did, making money trading digicreds for Tix and back again... Or coding apps... But J'ka liked to walk, to breathe air and to... Well... Be human.

What money he had was enough for now anyway. Not enough to be happy with, but enough to try. He had the flat, he had a killer stereo, a macrodeck and a spousel to keep him company. The spousel had been making supper, and the place smelt of spices.

"I thought tonight was going to be Parisian" he said as he walked in. He eyed the suspicious looking sauce and threading that boiled in the pot together. It looked strangely like rice noodles. He hated rice noodles.

"User has not provided adequate supplies. User needs to provide spousel with proper grocery list if user expects spousel to prepare adequate diet".

"Shut up! This is fine," he grumbled.

"When user next prepares grocery list..."

"I said shut up".

J'ka walked into his study (as he called it) and sat down. Though there was no actual separation of rooms in his flat (for it was one big room), he felt that he could create rooms, as long as he treated them that way. He had even had programmed the spousel to respond to distances as well as doorways within the flat.

"Food is now ready." the voice from the spousel came, it's voice muffled, as if it were behind a door (programming again).

J'ka walked thru the fake doorway, grabbed the plate and returned to the study.

Spousel followed him in.

He eyed the machine suspiciously. It hovered without noise, and was at the ready to clean his plate if he was done, or bring in a second helping if he wasn't. He wasn't having any of it. It really pissed him off that spousels were not given the rights that other robots were. If he let his outside, it would be grabbed up and taken for parts. Shame really. The bot industry deserved better.

"Power down cycle. Leave lights on. Return to grid".

Spousel chirped. "User has not yet fulfilled sexual activities and/or entertainment requirements for the evening. User must keep a steady program of..."

"Override! Shut the... Shut up!" He paused, then added: "And do the dishes in the morning!"

The spousel looked at him for a SEC, stared blankly, then shut off. The auto-return sequence switched on, and spousel slid over to the 'kitchen' corner and stood quiet. That always annoyed him, because it went through three 'walls' on the return path. He sighed, reached into his pocket, and pulled out the coin.

The instant he held it up to his face, it *tweanked*. At least, that's how he best described it. A *tweank*. Almost like a twinkle and a beep, or a wink and tweet... *Tweank*. It did it again and the room shook. Well, not really the room, but the entire building. A low rumble and then a loud clatter vibrated thru the whole scraper.

What the heck? The coin blinked and flashed and was about to physically leap out of hand, it was vibrating so much. He tried to stand, but lost his balance and fell out of the chair onto the floor. Rice noodles and sauce became airborne and hit the side table, clattering to the floor. Sauce was everywhere. He clenched both hands down around the coin and held it with all his might. What in the world? Items were flying off his shelves... It was chaos. Suddenly, just as it had begun, it all stopped.

Quiet. The only sounds were that of the various motion alarms going off around the scraper, and the tiny trickle of dust that was coming from the ceiling.

There was a hum and the spousel was at his side. It must have been knocked off the hook from the shaking. It turned to him.

"Give me the chip, J'ka," said the spousel in the factory setting voice. "It is important." The spousel held out its gear hand, fingers outstretched.

J'ka, on one elbow, slowly handed the spousel the coin.

"This?" he asked.

"None other." the spousel said, and placed the coin into its input tray.

"I'm sorry about all this." the spousel said.

It reached out its gear hand and hugged J'ka close.

Then out coiled its vacuum-like sexual appendage and inserted it into J'ka's mouth. Turning on the suction full power, it observed J'ka's death with a remorseless *tweank*.

J'ka slumped dead to the floor.

Spousel raised itself to full height and walked out the door, into the quiet of the building.

Older Twins

Maybe I would just call it "Snickerdoodle Vomit". A light brown, sure - but I hadn't seen this exact color in such a large area before. I supposed that I've seen most colors, but when you define them down to a single number, it was somehow satisfying. I didn't have the exact Pantone number for it, but it was something like 16-1234. Maybe that wasn't even a color in Pantone, I don't know... But were I working for a company and was forced, I would call it Distant Desert Deluge. Honestly, the color didn't even matter really, what was the important part was what was happening inside the building. It's just that I had a thing for color and liked to memorize them. A particular habit, but then again, I was a pretty particular guy. Inside the building was my girlfriend, I just hadn't met her yet.

"Dude, come on. It's going to be epic," Jake had told me. And I had come, even though it was in an older building.

The Big Event had happened around ten years ago, and it was pretty standard for larger buildings to be affected. As was the great fear when I was a kid, I had the chips put into my hands, feet and behind my ears. "Mark of the beast" the churches had screamed and some of them didn't get chipped. They changed their minds when they lost their identity from what the media called Twin Dissociation Syndrome. My parents were rich enough and wise enough to get me and my brother chipped early on.

I remember my brother and I were still going to public school where some people had been chipped and some hadn't. Kids would show up twice and other kids wouldn't show up at all. The worst thing was when a twin showed up, and the real kid didn't. You could always tell, but the twin would insist that they were the kid - The real kid. They would have the memories somewhat down, they would look alright, but you always knew.

Chauncy was my best friend in school and he was killed by his twin. I remember the day that I found out from his parents. My brother Jake and I had been pulled from school that very afternoon and were enrolled at one of the newer schools who only accepted those that had taken the chip.

Later that year when my brother and I came home from school, our mother was in the front lawn covered in blood. My brother's twin lay before her, full of holes from a kitchen knife. She had lived but would never be the same. We moved soon after. Our mother recovered (with scars), but the mental damage had been worse than the physical. Some days I would catch her looking at my brother before she would burst into tears and would have to leave the room.

I stood outside my parents' bedroom listening in on her talking to my father.

"I can't do it. I just can't make it go away," she said.

"It wasn't him. It wasn't anyone's child. It was a monster and you did the right thing." He tried to give her comfort.

"It was someone's child!," she screamed. "It was someone's child!" Over and over again, as we drove her to the hospital.

Was it someone's child? There were several opinions about them that I knew of. The largest group of people (at least, all the television shows), believed they were just like us, from another place. Another dimension. But that's not what the State and Federal laws reflected. Not in the least. Lobbyists from every nook and cranny were still trying to get the laws changed, but it was slow in coming.

When my mother killed my brother's twin, they asked her some questions, filled out some paperwork, but that was it. Animal control came and took away the body.

Animal control. Like it was a raccoon. I mean, it probably had more soul than a raccoon... They could *think* and everything. Not all the way, I mean, but mostly. Even now, I make it a habit of talking to the safe ones.

"Hi! How are you?" I ask.

A blank stare, a slow blink, "Hungry," a twin may reply.

"Want some of my sandwich?" I'll ask.

Another blank stare, then a look at me, then a hesitant and outstretched hand. It's then that I don't know what to expect. Usually I will put the sandwich down and slide it towards them. I don't like getting too close. Nobody does. Public Bus drivers had some of the first problems, and now most of them recognize how to deal with it. The Transit Authority of Omaha Nebraska were the first ones to figure it out. The twins loved to be around people. Not interacting with them, but just being around them. Staring at them, watching them, just being all-around creepy. So, they naturally will congregate at bus stops. They usually never have any money, and when they do, they usually don't know how to use it. Paying for the smallest things with wadded up hundred dollar bills, wherever the hell they would get them, who knows?

But anyway, so they get on the busses and cause a commotion, not understanding the tokens or routes, they just stand there and don't pay, or pay too much, not feeding it into the automated bill collector. Omaha inserted a Plexiglas into the back third of their bus, and told the twins to enter and exit by the back door. Well, they technically took off the door, but they did paint the entryway bright yellow and green and the twins get on and get off whenever they feel like it. I watched a selfie the other day about it.

"Oh it's weird all right," a large man in his forties was saying. "They just sit there and stare at you for the whole trip."

A bus driver was interviewed as well. "Yeah - so we just drop em off at the police station at the end of the day. Otherwise some of them would probably still be on the bus all night."

Worldwide, the Transit Authority of Omaha Nebraska "formula" caught on and tolerance seemed to be the best solution.

But the rest of the world is not Nebraska. It's a blessing and a curse for some countries. Greece enslaves all they can and puts them to work, even after their collapse, they still managed to figure things out. Russians shoot them on sight. Here, in the United States of America, mostly they are tolerated. India ignores them, I don't understand how, but in India there are not as many as there are here.

Scientists call them Homo Sapiens Idaltu after the men that were found at Herto, Ethiopia - Man's closest relative. I didn't like it. I believed something other than most. That they are not humans... That they are without mothers.

I was a child of the imagination, and therefore given to more fanciful thoughts. Though I've read everything I can on them, I still had a thousand questions. Were they from another place? Another dimension? Were they equal to humans? I believed that they weren't. That everything in them screamed out *"ALIEN"* to me was beyond doubt. Somehow, these entities were (in my mind) from another planet... But that's beside the point.

The building, as I was saying, was Snickerdoodle Vomit in color. It wasn't far from my dorm. I had gotten through school with passing marks and had wound up at Penn State. It was my second year. The world had changed and I guess I had changed along with it. Twins were now "resident aliens", legally here, and there was even a representative for them in the White House. Doctor Givvens. The real Doctor Givvens was a retired judge from Baltimore and apparently had given his consent to let his twin represent the others at some national level.

Jake called me in the parking lot. I answered. Yes I was here. Yes I was coming up. He was so pushy sometimes. I walked up the long porch way to the front door. "Closed for private event" it said. I opened the door.

"Here for the party?" A woman entirely in green asked as I walked into the vestibule.

"Yeah I guess." I told her. I cocked my head, unsure of myself. "What kind of party is this anyhow?" It was supposed to be a "safe" party.

She gave me a quick up and down. "You'll be fine dear," and began to talk on her phone. I hadn't noticed she had it in her hand. She turned away conferring with a friend. The front area of the building had been converted into the party-goers landing zone. A sign-in sheet was there if you wanted to get private referrals, e-mail sign up, a drawing for a fitness club.

The kind of things you expected at a big company get-together. That sounded just like my brother.

After high school, Jack had gone straight into a broker's apprenticeship and I hadn't heard from him in several years. He sent me cards on my birthday, and one on my graduation from high school. I knew that the birthday cards weren't signed by him, but the graduation card was. Along with a debit card for four thousand dollars. It made my dad mad but there was nothing he could do about it really. It was in my name... And I needed the money. Mom had been committed to an institution two years before and it was just him and I at the house, never on speaking terms.

I pushed the elevator button and waited. More guests were showing up, better dressed than I was. I had on a polo and chinos and my Rockport Pro Walker 9000's. This was as dressed up as I came. The elevator dinged and I got on, not bothering to hold the door. They were too busy chatting it up with the hostess anyway. The doors closed and the elevator lit up one button on the grid. The penthouse. I pushed it and it took me up.

I hadn't been this high in a long time. Around three hundred feet in the air, you really began to feel the effects of the resonation. It's why no one flew anymore. It's why radio didn't work and all signals bounced off of ground relays or better yet, used land and underwater cables. It's why no one went into tall buildings. But here I was, going to the penthouse. God help me, I'd better not tell my mom about this. She would have an episode and have to be sedated.

Pretty soon I was already experiencing the effects. I hadn't been this high since I was sixteen on a dare. I had gone into one of the buildings downtown and climbed the stairs. It was the most terrifying thing that I had ever done. I didn't even make it forty stories up. At floor thirty seven, I had experienced a seizure and my friends had called the fire department. The police were called and my father had almost beat me to death. That was years ago. That was when Mom was institutionalized.

They still didn't have a name for all the things you experienced when you were this high up. I had read "The official story." How no one wanted to attempt a rescue at the International Space Station. They had let them all die. There was nothing to do. They said that JAXA had sent up probes in an attempt to capitalize on it, but it was lost. Little by little, NASA and the USAF were dismantled and shared among the Navy and the Army. It didn't matter really. Whether NASA went into the Sea like the rumors said or whether they just quit the program completely didn't affect the common man like me. Right now, I was stuck in an elevator that was humming.

The buttons, the walls and even my jacket, began to become fuzzy. I was almost at the top. I wonder if all the clothes fell off, or were you just blurry. I was having a hard time focusing on everything, how sometimes things become blurry and double-visioned. Like that, but without the mental instability. This is how a crazy person must feel. Trapped inside of a body that is doing things on its own, when the consciousness remains intact. Maybe... It would have to be a specific type of crazy I guess. It was beyond me. I wasn't a psychoanalyst.

The button dinged at the top floor and the door opened. It wasn't really what I was expecting, but then again, I had no expectations. Some of the same logos that were at the bottom floor had smeared their signs here and there. When I say smear, I mean it. Ink didn't work up here like it did on the ground. You could write deep, or into something... Similar to how you could not only impress the news type into a ball of Silly Putty, but you could impress into it as well with grooves and gouges. The ink from the advertisements floated in mid-air like opulent cotton candy clouds. I walked right through them.

They were there - people I mean, walking around with garments that couldn't exist in real life. Larger than possible, colors that couldn't work. Angles that weren't supported by physics. And some of them were swimming through the air like it was water. I was hallucinating I decided, and dedicated my eyes to the floor and walked until I came to a wall, where I stopped, sat down, turned around and placed my back up against it.

I almost fell out of the building, and I would have if a hand hadn't grabbed me and pulled me back.

"Woah Nelly!" The voice said. It wasn't my brother, but a red-head with hair that was on fire. I wasn't alarmed by it, because it didn't appear to be real fire, but it was interesting to look at, nonetheless. I wanted to speak to her but all I could get out was a groan.

"Oh honey! Are you alright?" She offered me her hand to stand up. I waved her off and stayed on the floor. Not leaning on the wall, but not moving. I couldn't look up. The walls were waving like coral in the sea and it was very unnerving to say the least. I didn't know anyone and they didn't know me. Where was my brother when I needed him? The woman with the red hair hadn't left my side, instead she was looking at me with a cocked head. She squatted down and came eye to eye with me.

"Ohmygod, this is your first time, isn't it?" she asked, wide eyed. She knew it was, everyone knew it was, there was no hiding it. Definitely my first time for whatever this was. Going this high.

My brother never showed up. I eventually did stand up and hung out with Blackstar all night… That's what she said her name was. We talked, we danced and things got a little crazy when my twin showed up. Either Blackstar had slipped me something in my drink or it was just the way things were up here, but I sort of came to with my hands cuffed to a lamp post in the park. It still looked like we were on the top floor, but I couldn't be sure of anything anymore.

"No hard feelings man." he said. "I just wanted to meet you and I didn't think you'd be too keen on me coming down there. Not after what your mom did to my brother.

"Your broth…" I stammered. For some reason I couldn't speak.

"Yeah. Who did you think he was?" My twin scrutinized me, then sighed, placed a hand on my shoulder. "Sorry it had to come to this man. Really I am." I looked into his eyes and saw what I thought might be compassion. At least he looked the way I look when I mean it.

Despite myself, I smiled back. I couldn't really talk. It seemed I didn't know how. Things were strange here and the way things worked didn't work the way I wanted them to. I was aware that we were walking towards the bus station.

"…all like the bus station so much," my twin was saying with wonder. He was genuinely curious. "It's as if you really want to be going somewhere but don't really know where." he continued. How was there a bus station in the Penthouse I wondered. I also realized that I was incredibly hungry.

"Hungry…" I managed.

"Of course, how silly of me," my twin said, and handed me the bag he had been carrying. It had two sandwiches in it and a pickle in a Ziploc. I looked down at it blankly and got on the bus as they waved goodbye I could only think to myself: "What?"

When the Big Event came, they knew all about it. For years the scientists had told us that there were only this many months and this many days to be ready for it. They had warned us of possible outcomes and circumstances that may occur to us when it came. They had told us all the data, and we were all still afraid for our lives. In AD 2244 when event TG135 flattened the firmament, the impact decimated all life. We were left behind, in the mythosphere, as a remnant. An apology from God for the way things turned out.

The replacement Earth that God had built was much more safe and had every peace of mind ready and available for the humans left behind on the old one. They could feel free to live their lives and do what they needed to do without feeling overwhelmed or burdened, but the sky would be closed to them. Instead, the newer version Earth would be slowly placed down over the old one, until the meld was complete. It would be tricky at first, but He assured us that everything would work out in the end.

The good news is that we all got to ride the bus.

Poems

Shore #12

The wake I wake is not from dream
I feel the fall, Inhale the steam
I drift the drift that lovers dare
And when I fall, you will be there

You, joy eternal are my dance
Lift me up higher than any trance
Awake inside my tides recede
Awashed anew, you are my creed

Loss

I was yelling at the old man of the sea
Telling him to rightfully give back to me
I did not know that he had won you fair and square
I had no knowledge of your bet with that old man
I would let you go much easier my friend
Had I known of your old bet with that old man
I am cursing at the old man of the sea

Free to Decide

Fearless and free we change ourselves
    to become more than we could have imagined
Our lives become a small stone
    Washed upon the shore of limitless supply
As we stand in the horizon of our fortune

And look back on accomplishments forsaken
We mentally see our past and imagine a future
    Less provocative than we have ever seen
Full of choice and futile hope we realize
    that the choices desired are often destroyed
Fearless and free We free ourselves
    Fearless and free we heal ourselves
Let no man rule your destiny
Let no man rule your life


```
                                More Wind
                            and another
                            Breath of God
```


The dawn broke
out over the town
and the trees celebrated
the glory of it

The day cried out
Here I am
and the fog lifted
despising it

The birds sang happily
and sun streamed into
my musty bedroom
illuminating it

And I awoke
remembering the past
and the dreams vanished
like the night-time

The day was upon me

The moon had vanished
and the glory of God
had been reborn
upon the Earth
once again


```
               ...feeling and shut
```


Lazy hands make lazy work
Lazy feet and lazy play.
Lazy, lazy I feel so lazy.
Lazy's how I feel today.
Sunburnt and lazy. Sleepy and tired.
I'm sublime and quiet today.
Lazy face and lazy hands.
Lazy kings and lazy lands.
I can almost hear the bumblebees.
They are humming over the meadow.
Eyelids shut. My jaw hangs down.
Lazy, lazy days.

I cannot move.
I am too slow.
I feel so lazy.
The feeling never leaves.

I look at those poor tired old bees.
My hair is cut short.
It does not want to grow.
It is too lazy.

My beard is long.
My sword is sharp.
My sword is drawn.
But I am so lazy.

I am too lazy.
Too lazy today.

Of traitors and of thieves

Everywhere I go, someone knows your name.
Everywhere I go, I find your eyes.
Everywhere I go, I see your peace.
Everywhere I go, you shine like stars.
Every person I meet, needs your life.
Every idea that's thought, guides me to you.
Every theory unproven, proves your justice.
Every traitor you catch, trades you for silver.
Every moth that flies, does so by your grace.
Every rabbit that lives, does so on your prairie.
Every owl that sees, does so with your eyes.
Every woman that pains, gives birth to your love.
Every framer that frames, if only for art.
Every potter that spins, if only for water.
Every candle maker, if only for light.
Every thief that steals, if only for money.

Every creation bears your birthmark.

Save one.

Man
bears
your
name.

Love over

As the clock chases time for miles upon miles,

I sit on the grass and think about smiles.
For a time and a half, I ate a giraffe,
That I bought at an animal whale of a sale.
My shoes are now red, so I gave them away,
And the river was cool, so I drank like a fool.
Love over. My soul was under your love. Love over.
Just once I would like to be as loud as I might,
Like a solar flare burst could be bright.
But over again, I would just like to sit.
I would love to grow wings, and test out my strings,
And carve my whole name in the sky.
Love over. Red Rover. Send your love right over.
I know life is small, I have bugs on my wall.
But I can't leave a wake, it would be a mistake.
As my cat chases twine, as my brain does unwind,
I think about slime, and am I still fine?
Love over. And over. Love over.
The sunset of your love has begun.
My toes were under the sun.
Love lower.
Quite lower.
Love over.

                                        stardrop

under the drone of the bees

and the gray olive tree

when i heard you sing of

your sadness

for the writ which was lost

and the pain of the cost

and the smiles which did spring

from your pen

but like abraham's seed

like that promise indeed

are the stars ever seen

in the daylight

so look not to the left

to what was left behind

but cling to the promise you

believe in

are the stars ever seen

in the daylight

Essays

Gloria Tommamichael

This might be the hardest part of telling who I am and how I came to be in the entire book. The reason that I chose to put this chapter here will become clearer as you read, for Gloria knew me at the end of my confusion period and grew to love me all the way through the periods of my life that is this entire book.

Chronologically her chapter would either the first or the last in this small autobiography, but by placing it here I hope to have a common theme as a writer to show her involvement from first to last. I guess we have to go back to our series of events that led up to our meeting.

I had moved across Indiana from Ft. Wayne to West Lafayette at the suggestion of a lifelong friend, Roger Fletcher. Roger had the brotherly love enough to call me in Ft. Wayne and tell me that it was in my best interest to leave town in come live with him. I could share his apartment with he and his roommate and life would take on a new step. So I did, feeling like a new born. I had an intense desire to be brought back into the things that life had to offer. That I had been in complete misery in Eastern Indiana, I soon found joy and happiness in Western Indiana. I lived in country squire apartments, which was located next to where I worked as well as where I went to church.

The church quickly embraced me and I found a love from pastor Jeff Johns that I had not felt in quite a long time. Ted, the pastor of Green Pastures Christian Center, showed me that life could look up no matter what my circumstances showed. And as I began to volunteer my time there, I found happiness like I had only dreamed before. My tale of the church involvement has been a song of woe in my past as I have been ostracized, fired, denounced and even ex-communicated from several churches. I was relieved and overjoyed at their acceptance at Green Pastures.

I soon began singing in their worship group. As a progressive church with a full drum kit, guitars, and backup singers, I felt right at home. I even became their primary percussionist for a season. I loved music and loved to help out the band wherever they saw fit. That's where I saw Gloria for the first time....

It was New Year's Eve in 2000. Y2K was on most people's minds but not mine. As I looked out over the congregation there to usher in the New Year, I saw her singing and having a good time with the rest of the folk, love at first sight. Or first glance, or whatever. All I knew was I wanted that woman.

And eventually I had her. More than an encounter, more than a love, Gloria and I soon became part of a larger mind. A common theme. It felt as though we were meant to be together, and when we were together everything was al right. I don't know if you have ever felt the attraction physically but mentally as well as a connection that could not be explained, but there it was. Suddenly I felt as if I had found my lost twin.

And we married. It really wasn't how it should have been. We were hanging out on the morning of September 11,2001, just minding our own business when her mother called in hysterics. "Turn on the TV, Turn it on! Everyone's dying!"

And as we watched, I imagined everyone in their places around the world watching the same thing and saying the same thing: "Dear God, No." But there it was. The world was collapsing. So, Gloria logically figured that we should finalize things before anything else happened to us.

"Wanna get married?" And so it goes. Well at the same time the ink from her divorced husband wasn't even dry at this time. But she had moved away from Indianapolis to West Lafayette to get away because they were just done with each other. Gloria, the mother of three had packed up, relocated and started a new life, without him.

A note to the reader:

At this point in my writing, the man is incarcerated and will remain so for years to come for selling drugs to minors, his name will go unmentioned but the point will remain...Inability to cope brings us into a point in our minds when decisions that would have, at one point, been easy to say "no" to... suddenly are the snare that lands us in a world of discomfort. When we take the easy way out, not the right way out.

End note.

So Gloria and her three children became my new life. We learned, we grew, and we moved to Oklahoma to be closer to my family. We struggled, we survived. We struggled until we thrived. Patience and perseverance had its work until we found ourselves with two cars in the condo of our choice, with a great school for the kids and free schooling for her.

But the snag was it wasn't what we needed. Gloria was the breadwinner of the home making nearly three times my wages. Plus she was in school at nights so that left myself to play "Super Dad" with the kids.

Ladies: "Super Dads" are a great thing if you can get your hands on one. There's only one drawback. They sometimes have a martyr complex. This generally means that the martyr in the relationship has placed their partner on a higher status or perhaps a pedestal. They have given their "superior" partner permission to walk on, take advantage of, and treat them as if they were a doormat. The martyr feels justified in becoming the low one because either they honor their spouse with a false sense of hype-importance or they feel justified in being the lesser of the two in the relationship.

Now please don't be offended if you are a super dad (or super mom) and are healthy in your relationship with your partner. I am not describing you. I am describing a few unfortunate fellows of whom I was one. So I did everything. Fixed every problem, (battled every nighttime monster) cleaned every mess, cooked every meal, and Mama came home to me passed out on the couch with unfolded laundry all around me. The kids would already be in bed, kissed,
 re-tucked, and pronounced loved and she would help me finish folding the clothes and we would both collapse into bed.

For me, the process began five hours later and for her eight ours later. And so it goes.

Well let me just say that without respite, people go nuts. And we did. We tried self-help books, we tried church meetings, we tried modern relaxation techniques, and we even tried different sexual positions.

Nothing helped. So, finally sick of never seeing her own kids, she came home and told me…

"I'm leaving."

"Oh, okay, when are you coming back?"

"No, I'm…Leaving"

"Leaving?"

"Leaving."

And so we began our ping-pong lifestyle on and off affair that lasted over five years. There were ups and downs, there were on and offs, but in the end it was off, and we both knew it, but neither one of us wanted to admit it.

So after dumping the lease, selling the stuff, getting it all hauled away and packing my car, my three-bedroom condo was a thing of the past and I followed her back to Indiana.

In Indiana we reconciled. Several times actually I would call her and call her and she would play hard to get. And then there would me a month or two of silence, and then voila she would call me and call me and I would play hard to get and, over and over the cycle would go.

But in the end we actually spent more time as friends than enemies. After coming back to Tulsa before the last time we reconciled I had sworn to never love her again.

But I had not buried the inevitable. You see, for much of my life I have kept the words "destiny" out of my everyday vocabulary. Now I still do not use this word as a rule, but I will use it here. "Destiny" is not the inescapable future (as in the dooming harbinger of a hellish life) but the unstoppable ending (as in a glorious reward for a job well done.) No one should ever misinterpret their destiny as a hammer in the sky destruction of implement. But rather see destiny as only the trophy for whatever outcome your life yields.

No destiny was (as far as my chase after Gloria is concerned) realizing that if I choose to, I could race around the track at 300 miles an hour only to burn out one day in a ball of blazing fury... or, I could choose to slow down, take a right turn off the course and quit the race altogether much as a NASCAR driver might decide to pilot an airplane for a career change. I realized that the entire sport was incorrect. I once told Gloria (in one of our thousands of long-distance phone calls) that the only word to describe her was ineffable, "which is hard to explain." I told her that I would buy her a billboard and proclaim it to the world. Well I did have a hard time explaining what she did to my heart and my brain, but the only thing to do was bow my head in respect, recognizing defeat, and walk away.

Now there is a story of this very element of self-awareness that springs to mind. The story goes that during the days of the Shogun Samurai, in Japan, there happened to be a very narrow road in a wood and two Samurai were traveling on it at the same time, in fact the others town to kill him. They were each headed in the opposite direction headed towards each other on the same road and met at a bridge. The first Samurai stood on the western side of the bridge and the second Samurai stood on the eastern side of the bridge. And the stood. Waiting. What were they doing? Waiting, watching, and evaluating the other. Finally after several hours of meditation of the others being, they almost simultaneously bowed to each other. Snapped about, and walked back to their own respective village. The moral? Arriving at intimate knowledge of another can come in many ways, but the most important thing is that you do arrive. And once you've arrived make a decision. The Samurai were each masters of their own rights, and know that to battle one another would only lead to the death of both of them. So respectfully and wisely they each decided to give the other the honor of a full and healthy life and walk away from the situation in tact.

Another lesson, and this one a more western and modern realization...to live! To walk away when you know you're beat. Retreat, regroup, rethink, replan, re-evaluate. To stop what you're doing and plot another course of action.

Only the fools and impetuous charge the bull in a fight.

Into Gehenna without a Paddle

Within a year I had gone from "Mister Awesome" to "Something like a Monster." My wife had indeed gotten pregnant from her new boyfriend and I think I must have lost my mind because for a year there I went from being on top of the American Church Game to being a low-life sinner. I filled my days with sex from strangers, getting high and drinking. I started smoking cigarettes, started not caring about the shop and eventually I didn't even live at my house any more. I let some homeless people move in and took over my new girlfriend's lease while she joined the Navy. I lost the lease on the coffeeshop, put everything in storage and took a job down the street as a waiter and bartender. I totaled my car, and was soon kicked out of my apartment because I ended up getting roommates that ran me away from there as well.

And then, My Step-Mother died. That was it. That was the last straw. I decided to kill myself. I filed a quit-claim on my house and kicked out my roommates to the apartment. I had my wrecked car towed away and gave up on the storage unit. I ditched the job and stayed at my apartment. I had $400 left to my name. The phone rang. It was Pletch from Harvest Christian. He told me that God had appeared to him and told him to call me. He told me that if I didn't leave that I would die. I told him: "Let me pray about that." I hung up the phone and picked up the bible. It fell open at Joel chapter two, verse three: "A fire devours before them; and behind them a flame burns: the land is as the Garden of Eden before them, and behind them a desolate wilderness; yea, and nothing shall escape them." I called him back. "When can you be here?" I asked. "Two hours." He said. "Come get me." I said, and hung up.

I left it all. I brought four boxes full of old journals and photo albums and a backpack full of clothes. I didn't contact the landlord, didn't tell anyone, I just left. You know. Maybe the biker gang I had a tangle with was coming for me. Maybe my old business partner at the bar I started would have taken me out. Maybe some of the *Left Path Satanists* that almost burned down my home would have done me in. Maybe it would be the Wiccans who used to curse me as I worked at the shop. Maybe it would have been my wife's boyfriend and his posse. Maybe it would have been Jim's family coming after me. Maybe Timmy. Maybe I would have killed myself. I will never know. But I left Fort Wayne and never looked back.

www.ingramcontent.com/pod-product-compliance
Lightning Source LLC
Chambersburg PA
CBHW030153200626
46812CB00016B/1834